For Lex, Ginger, Bonny and everlasting George.

Published in 2020 by Melbournestyle Books
155 Clarendon Street, South Melbourne
Victoria 3205, Australia
www.melbournestyle.com.au

 A catalogue record for this book is available from
the National Library of Australia
National Library of Australia Cataloguing-in-Publication entry:

Coote, Maree, author, illustrator.

Dogography: The amazing world of letter art dogs /
Maree Coote, author, illustrator.

ISBN 978-0-6485684-1-4 (hbk.)

Subjects:
1. Graphic design (Typography) -- Pictorial works -- Juvenile literature.
2. Dogs -- Pictorial works -- Juvenile literature.
3. Alphabet in art -- Pictorial works -- Juvenile literature.
4. Animals -- Pictorial works -- Juvenile literature.
5. English language -- Alphabet -- Pictorial works -- Juvenile literature.
6. Visual poetry, Australian -- Pictorial works -- Juvenile literature.

Printed in China by C+C Offset Printing on wood-free paper

10 9 8 7 6 5 4 3 2 1

MELBOURNESTYLE
BOOKS
www.melbournestyle.com.au

FONTIGRAM

MAREE COOTE

DOGoGRAPHY

The Amazing World of Letter Art Dogs

LOOK-AND-FIND · EVERY PICTURE MADE WITH THE LETTERS OF ITS OWN NAME · SPELL-A-PICTURE

LETTER ART

Every part
of me's a letter
Does that help you
see me better?
Look very closely
and you'll see
The hidden letters
that spell me!

Sometimes
letters may repeat,
To make more eyes,
or ears or feet,
But back-to-front
or upside-down,
All my letters
can be found!

These are the letters that make the picture:

Pug

I'm gentle, loyal, fairly hairy,
If spelled correctly, not too scary.

These are the letters that make the picture:

GeRMAN ShePheRD

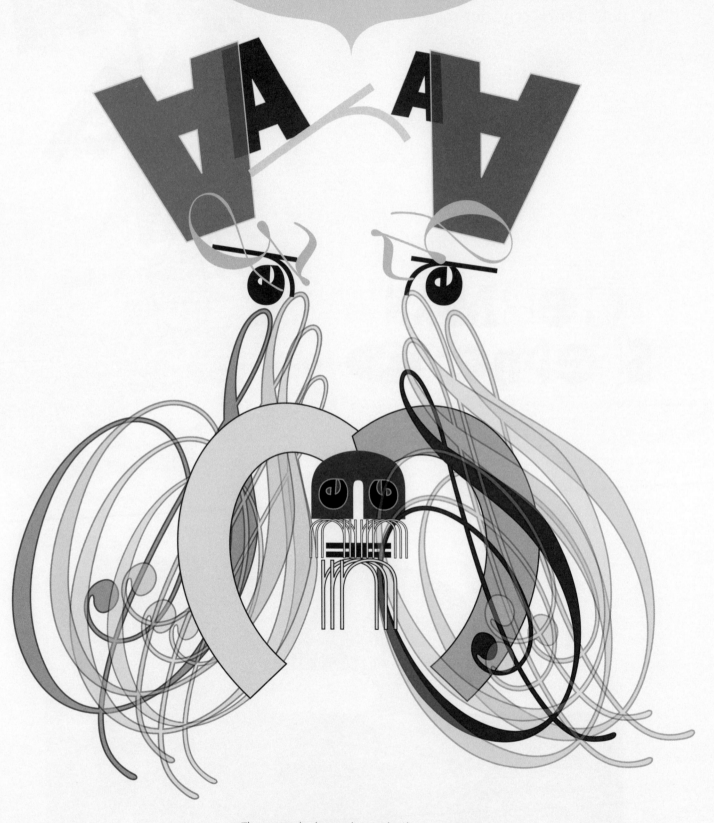

These are the letters that make the picture:

These are the letters that make the picture:

LABRADOODLE

You'll find these letters waddling 'round
About an inch above the ground.

These are the letters that make each dog:

DACHSUND

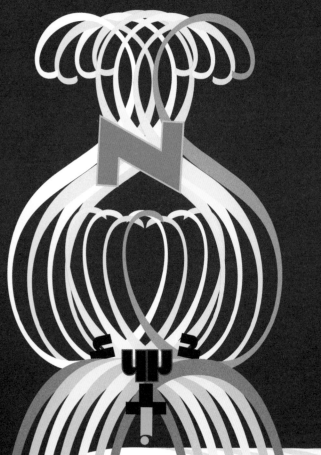

Spell me first,
then paint my nails.
And tie my hair
in pony tails.

These are the letters that make the picture:

Shih TZU

These are the letters that make the picture:

jACK russELL

Perfect spelling,
Perfect stance,
'Best in Show',
Made in France!

These are the letters that make each dog:

POODLe

These letters spell a brilliant swimmer,
Kind and gentle, could be slimmer.

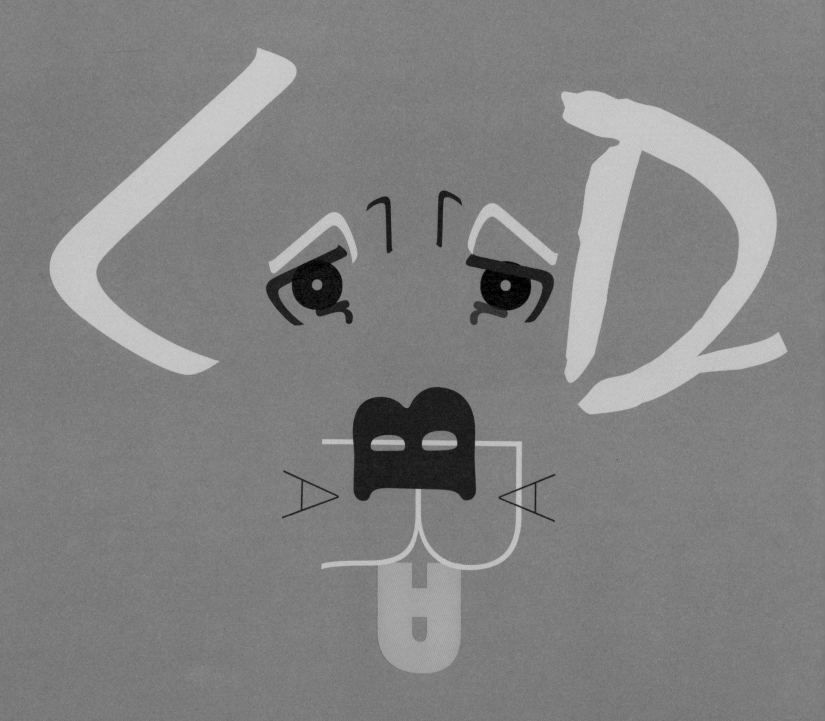

These are the letters that make the picture:

LABRADOr

Spots are boring!
— I prefer
that letters
decorate my fur.

These are the letters that make the picture:

daLmatiAn

The Queen of England's
favourite breed,
Neatly spelled, washed,
and de-flead.

These are the letters that make each pup:

corgi

These are the letters that make the picture:

ChiHUAHUa

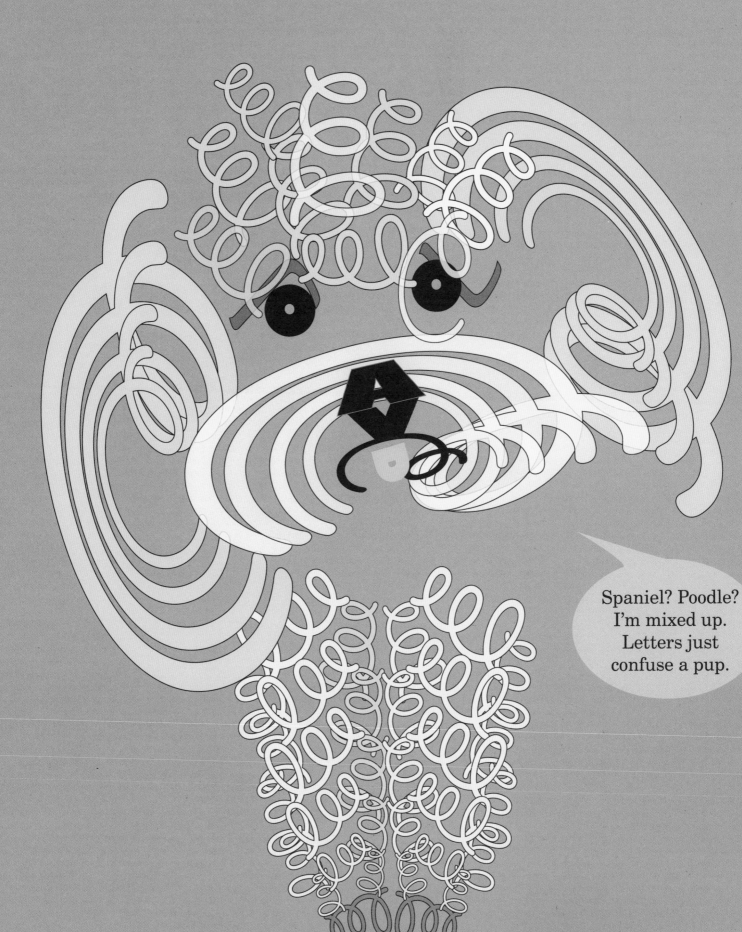

These are the letters that make each dog:

DOBERMAN

My letters spell
a small (but tough),
Tightly wound-up
ball of fluff!

These are the letters that make the picture:

POMERANIAN

These are the letters that make each pup:

mALteSe

I'm complicated...
Can you see?
How every letter
makes me
'Me'!

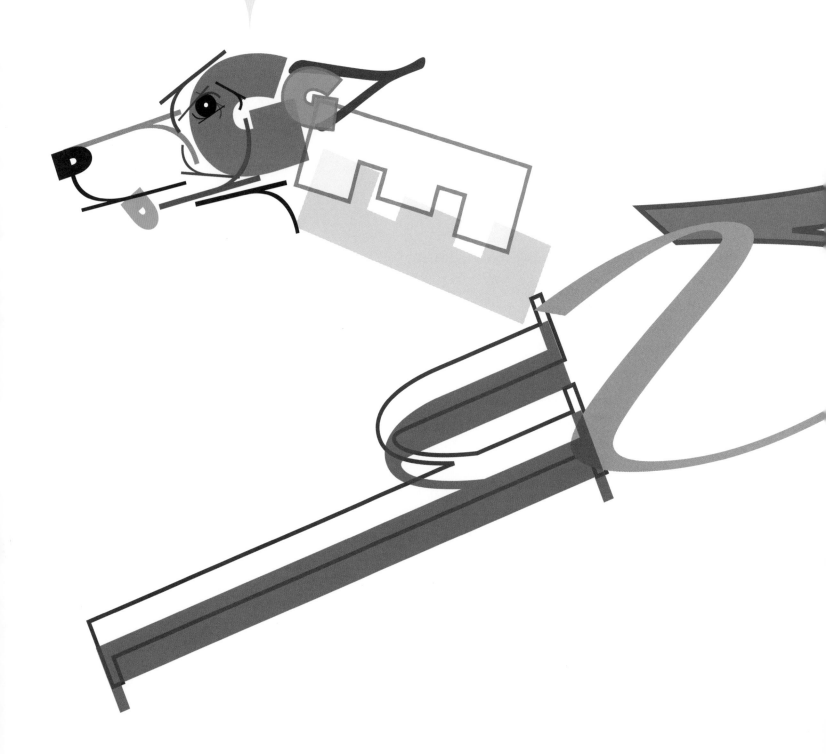

These are the letters that make each dog:

GrEYhOund

Such glamour in each gorgeous letter.
It's true! Redheads wear letters better.

These are the letters that make the picture:

iRiSH
setter

Slowly, I'll just sniff around, 'Til all my letters have been found.

These are the letters that make the picture:

BASSet hOUnD

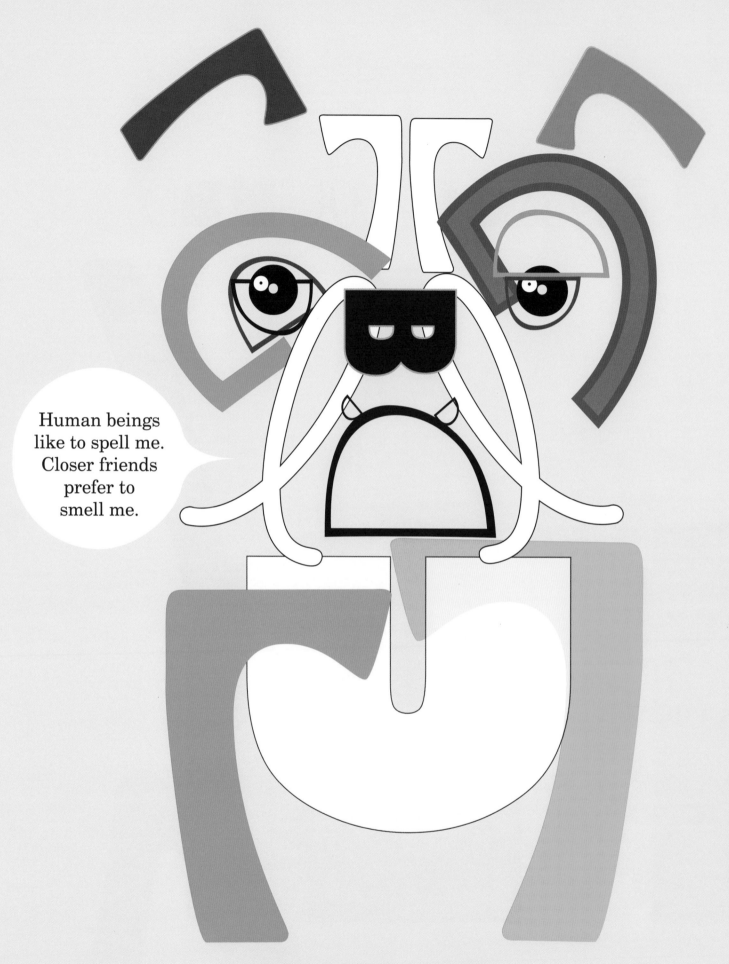

These are the letters that make the picture:

BUℓℓDOG

CLEVER KIDS TEACHERS' NOTES

ABOUT THIS BOOK & LETTER ART

Every picture in this book is made with the letters that spell each dog's name. Some letters may repeat for extra hair or feet. Each page has a 'letter key' which shows the exact letters and fonts that have been used to create each image. Find these letters in the image. What kind of dog do YOU have? Look closely at its features. Study the shapes in the letters of its name. Can you arrange them into a likeness of your pup?

ABOUT TYPOGRAPHY

A 'font' is a design for a set of letters of the alphabet. $\quad$ A A

A serif font has letters with little feet. A sans-serif font has letters without little feet. Can you find examples of letters in these font styles in this book:

| CAPITAL | lower case | Sans-serif | Serif |
| Regular | **Bold** | *ITALIC* | *Script* |

ABOUT DOG BREEDS

The amazing variety in dog appearance is due mostly to human interference by 'intentional selection'. Breeds are crossed for characteristics like heightened scent or sight, longer or shorter legs, snouts, or hair, certain behaviour or personality, and so on. The resulting offspring are then bred only within the same kind to create what is called a 'pure-bred', although this process is quite artificial.

A natural or mixed-breed is called a 'mongrel' or 'bitser', and is generally the result of 'natural selection', and not of intentional cross breeding.

The word 'puppy' comes from the French word 'poupée' meaning 'doll'.

. . .

The PUG is a 'companion dog' or 'lap dog'. Adopted into Europe in the 1500s. Origin: China, Song Dynasty, 960-1279.

The GERMAN SHEPHERD is a guard dog. Prior to 1977 it was known in the UK as the Alsatian. Origin: Germany, 1800s.

The SCHNAUZER's name translates from the German word for 'snout', and refers to the hairy muzzle of the breed. Origin: Germany, 1300s.

The LABRADOODLE is a crossbreed between labrador and poodle. Bred to provide a companion dog with a low-shedding coat. Origin: Australia, 1988.

The DACHSHUND's name means 'badger dog'. They were deliberately bred with short legs to chase badgers down burrows. Origin: Germany, 1500s. Earlier longer-legged breeds date back to ancient Egypt.

The SHIH TZU is a cross between a Chinese Pekingese and Tibetan Lhasa Apso. Popular as a 'lap dog'. Origin: China, late 1600s.

The JACK RUSSELL is a fox hunter, adept at burrowing. Origin: England, 1795.

The POODLE is the second most intelligent dog after the Border Collie. Origin is disputed: either from Germany in the 1500s, or France (Barbet), 1700s.

The LABRADOR is a companion dog, famous as a guide dog. An adept swimmer, it was originally known as St John's Water Dog. Origin: Canada, 1600s.

The DALMATIAN was used as a 'carriage dog', to trot beside horse-drawn cabs as a calming influence on the horses and as a status symbol. Origin: Croatia, 1600s.

The CORGI is a herding dog, originally used with cattle. Origin: Wales, 900s.

The CHIHUAHUA is known as a 'toy dog' and is the smallest of all dog breeds. Origin: Mexico, in the 1500s.

The CAVOODLE is a cross between a poodle and Cavalier King Charles spaniel. Origin: Australia, 1990s.

The DOBERMAN was bred as a fierce guard dog. Origin: Germany around 1890.

The POMERANIAN is a 'toy dog' or 'lap dog', popular in early European courts as a companion dog. Origin: Germany/Poland, 1700s.

The MALTESE is a 'toy dog'. Origin: Mediterranean region, from 500BC.

The GREYHOUND is a 'sight hound', using sight instead of smell to chase hare and deer. Later used as racing dogs. Origin: Eurasia, Roman period, 50-270AD.

The IRISH SETTER is used by hunters to 'set' its focus and point out the location of game birds hidden in the landscape. Origin: Ireland, early 1800s.

The BOSTON TERRIER is nicknamed the 'American Gentleman' for its black and white coat markings that resemble a gent's tuxedo. Origin: USA, 1893.

The BASSET HOUND is a 'scent hound' or 'blood hound', originally used for hunting hare and other game. Origin: France/Great Britain, late 1800s.

The BULLDOG gets its name from the way it was used up until the early 1800s in a gambling game of attacking bulls called 'bull-baiting'. Origin: England, 1800s.

MELBOURNESTYLE BOOKS
www.melbournestyle.com.au

CLEVER KIDS TEACHERS' NOTES about Letter Art, typography and this book are available at www.melbournestyle.com.au and www.cleverkids.net.au